WHAT'S HAPPENING

ON THE

Heather Amery
Illustrated by Stephen Cartwright

Consultant: Betty Root
Centre for the Teaching of Reading
University of Reading, England

Looking after the hens

How many eggs have the hens laid?

What is the horse doing?

Shearing the sheep

Which animal has run in with the sheep?

Can you find the lost lamb?

Looking at the pigs

How many pigs can you see? How many are

piglets?   Which animal is looking for food?

Feeding the ducks

How many ducklings are there?

Which duck cannot see much?

Milking time for the cows

Can you find a green frog?

Who is going to get wet?

Picking the apples

How many different animals can you see?

Who is eating the apples?

By the barn

Find 2 white hens and 3 mice.

What has happened to the trailer?

Match the mothers with their babies.

What are the baby animals called?

First published in 1984
Usborne Publishing Ltd
20 Garrick St, London
WC2 9 BJ, England
© Usborne Publishing Ltd 1984

Printed in Portugal

The name of Usborne and the device 🎈 are Trade Marks of Usborne Publishing Ltd.

All rights reserved. No part of this publication may be reproduced, stored in a retrieval system or transmitted in any form or by any means, electronic, mechanical, photocopying, recording, or otherwise, without the prior permission of the publisher.